Mel Bay Presents

New Dimensions in Classical Guitar for Children

By Sonia Michelson

MW00559139

Contents

2 3 4 5 6 7 8 9 0

© 1991 BY MEL BAY PUBLICATIONS, INC., PACIFIC, MO 63069.
ALL RIGHTS RESERVED. INTERNATIONAL COPYRIGHT SECURED. B.M.I. MADE AND PRINTED IN U.S.A.
No part of this publication may be reproduced in whole or in part, or stored in a retrieval system, or transmitted in any form
or by any means, electronic, mechanical, photocopy, recording, or otherwise, without written permission of the publisher.

Visit us on the Web at www.melbay.com — E-mail us at email@melbay.com

To my children—Ann, Louis, Hadassah, Julia,
Elise, Eliot, and Jack—
and to
all my musical children and their parents,
for their enthusiasm,
cooperation, and joyful spirit.

Only those who have the patience
to do simple things perfectly
Ever acquire the skill
to do difficult things easily.

—Schiller—

Contents

Introduction

It was the writings of Shinichi Suzuki and Zoltan Kodaly that inspired and led me to this new approach to teaching music and classical guitar to children. I have written this book so that other teachers may find success and pleasure in teaching young people.

Using a holistic approach to early childhood education, I have combined the Suzuki-Kodaly principles into a developmental method. Only one new idea or step is introduced at a time. When this is mastered, the child goes on to the next small challenge. Of foremost importance has been my awareness of each child's unique potential. Therefore, emphasis has been on stimulating each child's musical imagination and ability through special guitar techniques, eurythmics, listening games, and theory games. Students learn through participation in movement, singing, and guitar performance.

This method has been developed over a four-year period with my students and has been successfully used with children from age 3 through age 10. From the very first lesson, the emphasis is on performing music for others. My students actively perform in recitals, workshops, and concerts. I have even used this method successfully with some adults. Naturally this will depend on the individual and his or her musical background and experience.

It is assumed that you, as the teacher of this method, play classical guitar and know the basic fundamentals of good technique, including rest stroke and free stroke, with emphasis on a round, full tone. You should also know what constitutes correct hand positions and good sitting posture.

It is also important to realize that there are many ways to teach music and guitar. Each child is a unique individual, and flexibility in presenting these teaching ideas is of utmost importance.

The material covered in Levels I–V can be mastered in approximately one to two years. Initially the rote learning method is used in conjunction with the Curwen melodic hand signals to identify intervals. Children find joy in making music from the very first song. They develop round tone and a solid technique, acquire basic music fundamentals, and have the pleasure of singing and playing authentic folk songs, as well as playing good composed music.

I wish to express particular appreciation to Neil Mermelstein for his editing advice, and to Ana Bensinger, Christine Kelly, Susan Mallek, Janice McKibbin, Barbara Friedman, Thomas Pool, Andrea Saffir, Herb Emmerman, Margaret Mistak, Mark, and Avi Zohar for suggestions, encouragement, and critical judgment. Their help has been most valuable.

Acknowledgment is gratefully made to Livia Ayal, who introduced me to the philosophy and methods of Zoltan Kodaly. She encouraged me to use those ideas in teaching the classical guitar, thereby leading the way to this book. And acknowledgment is made to Jeanne Brazier for furthering my interest in Suzuki teaching, and to Douglas W. Smith for his innovative ideas in teaching the very young. And special thanks to my understanding students and their parents for encouragement to undertake this project.

I hope that this new approach to learning music will be useful to you in your teaching of classical guitar to children. It is our privilege as teachers to help children become more sensitive and to discover the joy and pleasure in music and, in doing so, enrich their lives.

Sonia Michelson

Principles for Successful Study

∞ The parent should have a positive attitude and be involved. This motivates the child toward effective home practice and is perhaps the most important principle. Each parent must have a strong commitment to help the child learn and must attend each lesson with undivided attention. In addition, the parent must help the child review continuously and be actively involved with music and practice at home.

∞ The teacher should present the pieces in the order given and use exact fingering. Following the sequence of pieces based on the pentaton (the five-tone scale—**do re mi so la**) will build solid technique and a good musical foundation.

∞ It is important that the teacher play the pieces for the student and record the pieces on a cassette tape. The student should listen to the taped pieces daily at home to develop musical sensitivity and become familiar with the melodies. Progress depends on this listening.

∞ A full, round tone, using a firm rest stroke, should be stressed from the very beginning.

∞ Constant attention should be given to correct posture and to right and left-hand positions.

∞ An important part of left-hand technique is to train all the student's fingers simultaneously. That is why the early pieces frequently use the often-neglected third and fourth fingers of the left hand. A balanced left hand is acquired from the earliest days of practice.

∞ Eurythmics (walking, marching, clapping, tapping to a rhythm) should be included at each lesson to develop a strong feeling for pulse and to keep the child's interest high.

∞ Children will enjoy singing the folk songs and should use the Curwen hand signals (see section on **Imaginative Games, Exercises & Teaching Ideas**) to visualize sound intervals in space and to indicate the movement of intervals within a melody. Inner ear training is extremely important and will enable the child to create a beautiful singing tone on the guitar.

Overview

This method is based on building musical knowledge and technical skill by introducing only one new step at a time. Since this approach uses the Kodaly interval system, it is important to start all students (ages 3–10) at the beginning of Level I with the song "Cuckoo" and proceed sequentially.

Younger children will normally take one to four months to play "Cuckoo." A child of 9 or older will usually proceed through Levels I–II in a much shorter time than a younger child.

The key of G and 2/4 meter are used extensively in the beginning pieces. Use of the weak third finger of the left hand from the very beginning will, with repeated use, strengthen that finger.

This method uses a movable-do system. In the key of G, the note D (**so**) on string 2 is the first note introduced in Level I, followed by B (**mi**) on string 2 to give a minor third (**so-mi**). Later, E (**la**) and G (**do**) are included to create the triad **so mi do.** Level II introduces A (**re**), completing the pentaton (**do re mi so la**). Not until Level III is C (**fa**) on the second string introduced with "Twinkle, Twinkle Little Star."

Level IV introduces the minor key in "Moon Magic" and pieces with more extended melodic lines, such as "Come Little Children" and "Simple Gifts." Level V pieces are more advanced, introducing dotted rhythms and syncopation, as in "Turn Again Whittington" and "Alabama Girl." The last two pieces in Level V, "Minuet" by W. A. Mozart and "Minuet in G" by J. S. Bach, require more musical phrasing and understanding.

Only when aural and digital skills are firmly established is the child introduced to reading. This is usually appropriate when Level III has been successfully completed.

The early lessons will help the child learn how to focus attention and concentrate. The child will also learn to follow directions and how to listen. And, of course, the beginning coordination of hands will enable the child to play easy pieces on the guitar.

Format

This book is divided into three main sections:

I. First Lessons

Here you will find explicit suggestions for teaching the early formative lessons. In subsequent lessons, you can follow a similar format.

Please note: Do not proceed to song 2, "One, Two, Tie My Shoe," until the child has mastered song 1, "Cuckoo." "See-Saw" and "Star Light" may be introduced after song 1.

II. Imaginative Games, Exercises & Teaching Ideas

In this section, you will find explanations of the exercises and games mentioned throughout the book. Games are tremendously important to children and should be included in each lesson. So much real learning in a child takes place in the name of play. These games make learning exciting and enjoyable. Most of the games can be used interchangeably with all the beginning pieces.

As Maria Piers wisely noted, *"The remarkable aspect of learning by play is that it is never lost. Later lessons acquired in school are forgotten, but the things we learn in play—hard but playfully won—we never forget."*

III. Pieces

Most pieces include a focus, a song, and expansion activities:

The **focus** indicates the musical or technical importance of the piece.

The **song** is given with simple melodic line, words, and chord symbols for accompaniment. From the beginning song, the teacher can accompany the student with a simple bass-chord or arpeggio pattern.

The **expansion activities** suggest useful games or explanations of technique. More games and activities are suggested in the early lessons than in the later lessons. As the child becomes more musical and can play the pieces with greater technical ease, the emphasis will be more on the music itself. These activities should be repeated at each of the early lessons until they are well learned. This will build the foundation for learning later lessons.

Ideas for Teaching Children Effectively

∞ Take one step at a time. Any child can play these pieces if they are given one at a time and practiced until mastered. This whole new approach focuses on learning in small steps. Only one musical concept (or technique) is introduced at a time.

∞ Involve the parents. This is extremely important. The parent should take notes at the lesson and help the child practice at home. The parent should also supervise the daily listening to the tape.

∞ For children under 6, a half-size guitar and capo should be used. A small chair, a regular guitar footstool, and a music stand should be provided.

∞ Maintain eye-level contact with your young student during teaching. This will hold the child's attention, and the child will not feel threatened by your height.

∞ Continue to **review** pieces at all levels. Use imaginative games such as Music Box or the Odd-Even Game.

∞ Be sensitive to the child's mood. Watch facial expressions, yawns, and wiggles. Be firm but sensitive and kind. Change to a different rhythm or piece quickly if the child is having undue difficulty. If the child does not seem eager to learn or seems confused, you probably are not presenting the material correctly.

∞ It is extremely important to understand and emphasize the difference between learning and practicing a piece. After a student has learned to play a piece correctly, then it must be practiced many times over with good tone and expression until it becomes internalized.

∞ Give the child performance opportunities. Plan monthly workshops and an annual recital to provide stimulation and growth. The child learns to polish and memorize a piece for performance, gains poise in presentation, listen to other children perform well, and enjoys being in a musical environment.

∞ Reward achievement. A child has a tremendous feeling of achievement upon being able to play all the pieces in Level I. Presentation of a Certificate of Merit to the child at the next workshop is highly recommended. A Certificate of Merit should then be presented as the child successfully completes each subsequent level. Success in playing one piece creates the inner drive for the child to want to continue learning music and the guitar.

∞ Work for excellence and encourage your students, praising them warmly and wisely. Always keep in mind that you want the children to love music and playing the guitar. Make lessons enjoyable!

Recommended Reading

Classical Guitar Study: A Guide for Teachers and Parents, Sonia Michelson, 1981, 1465 S. Reeves St., Los Angeles, CA 90035.

Nurtured by Love: A New Approach to Education, Shinichi Suzuki, 1969, Exposition Press, Inc., Jericho, NY 11753.

The Selected Writings of Zoltan Kodaly, ed. Ferenc Bonis, 1974, Boosey & Hawkes Music Publishers Ltd., Regent Street, London W1A 1BR, England.

The Kodaly Method, Comprehensive Music Education from Infant to Adult, Lois Choksy, 1974, Prentice-Hall, Inc., Englewood Cliffs, New Jersey.

The Suzuki Violinist: A Guide for Teachers and Parents, William Starr, 1976, Kingston Ellis Press, Knoxville, Tennessee.

The Suzuki Concept: An Introduction to a Successful Method for Early Music Education, ed. Elizabeth Mills and Sr. Therese Murphy, 1973, Diablo Press, Berkeley, CA 94707.

Kindergarten Is Too Late, Masaru Ibuka, 1977, Simon and Schuster, New York, NY 10020.

The Splendor of Music, Angela Diller, 1957, G. Schirmer, Inc., New York, New York.

The Twelve Lesson Course in a New Approach to Violin Playing, Kato Havas, 1964, Bosworth & Co., Ltd., Regent Street, London, W. I.

The Guitar from the Renaissance to the Present Day, Harvey Turnbull, 1974, Charles Scribner's Sons, New York, New York.

Guitar Study for the Pre-College Student: A Graded Curriculum (Levels I–II), Sonia Michelson, Margaret W. Mistak, and Douglas W. Smith, 1981, Dauphin Company, P.O. Box 5137, Springfield, IL 62705.

First Lessons

Ages
3–5
6–10

Sample Lesson Plans

These sample lesson plans are offered to stress the great importance of review and repetition. These lessons should proceed very slowly. It may take two to three weeks or more for very young children to learn each song.

Lesson One

1. Getting acquainted: This is a very new experience for your young student. Help put the child at ease. While you are tuning the guitar, you might suggest that the child make a drawing with crayons on some scratch paper you have set out on a corner table. This not only eases the tension of the first lesson and keeps the child busy for a few minutes, but it is also a good indication of how the child relates to his or her world through drawing.

2. Parents: Since parental involvement is extremely important right from the beginning, suggest that the parent take notes during the lesson. Supply a pre-recorded cassette tape of the pieces to be learned in Level I. Stress the great importance of the child's listening to the tape daily.

3. Standing-Still Game: Have the child assume a pre-bow posture with feet together and hands at the sides. See if the child can stand still to the count of 1–10 without moving. This is important for learning to follow directions.

4. Child Takes a Bow: Have the child stand upright at the count of 1, then bend at the waist at the counts of 2 and 3, and straighten up at the counts of 4 and 5.

5. Eurythmics: To have the child feel the 2/4 pulse, walk around the room with the child, saying "Left, right, left, right," etc., then "1, 2, 1, 2." Then sing "Cuckoo" while walking around the room clapping 1, 2, 1, 2. Tell the child that this 1, 2 is like a heartbeat. Then tap the pulse on a triangle (or other rhythm instrument) while walking around the room singing "Cuckoo."

6. Rhythm: Sing rhythm syllables and clap to melody of "Cuckoo":

| | | ⊓ |
ta ta ti ti ta

7. Play the Ball Game (Game No. 3).

8. Play Where Is Thumbkin? (Game No. 9).

9. Melodic interval syllables: Have the child sing "Cuckoo" with melodic syllables:

so   mi   so so mi

Then have the child sing "Cuckoo" using the melodic syllables **so mi so so mi** while using the proper Curwen hand signals.

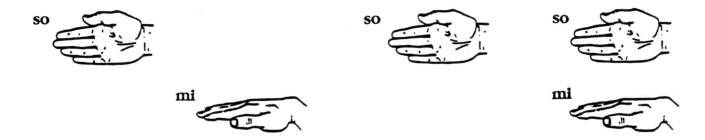

10. Play the Ready Game (Game No. 4).

11. Arm and hand positions: Place a capo on the guitar on fret VII or V and show the child how to sit correctly with the guitar. Then indicate the proper right-hand position: The thumb *(p)* and the first three fingers *(i, m, a)* are first placed on string 1 (E). Then *p* is placed on string 5 (A). This creates the correct curve to the fingers and wrist in relation to the strings.

If the child finds it too difficult to hold the guitar correctly at first, there is an alternative way to introduce the guitar: Place the guitar flat on a table (or the floor) with you and the child sitting in front of the horizontal guitar. Place the child's right-hand index finger *(i)* on string 1.

Note: It is important to use the term "pointer" for the index finger, since this is the term used in the song "Thumbkin" (Game No. 9). It makes it much easier for the child if you refer to the fingers of the right hand as "pointer" *(i)*, "middleman" *(m)*, and "ringman" *(a)*, at least through Level II.

The child is now ready to proceed to Exercise 1.

12. Exercise 1: Hold the child's index finger and carefully demonstrate a good rest stroke on string 1. Emphasize good tone. Do this a number of times with patience and praise. Then try the same motion with the middle finger. It is also a good idea to have the parent assume the sitting position and practice Exercise 1.

13. Play the On-Off Game (Game No. 5).

14. Exercise 2: When the child can perform Exercise 1 correctly, go to Exercise 2, alternating *i, m* on string 1. Then proceed to string 2 (B), alternating *i, m*. You are now ready to coordinate playing with both hands.

15. Play "Cuckoo" for the first time: The child plays "pointer-middleman" *(i, m, i, m)* with the right hand, while you place the child's third finger of the left hand on note D **(so)**. The child plays the note. Then the child removes the left-hand finger from the string and plays another note (open-string B). The result is **so-mi.**

Practice this many times with the child, always helping with the third finger of the left hand. The child can now play "Cuckoo" with your help. It is a very exciting moment! However, it will take many weeks before the child's finger is strong enough to play this alone.

A great deal of patience, praise, and encouragement for the young student (and for the parent, too) are needed and desired at this early stage.

16. Play the Listening Game (Game No. 6).

17. Child Takes a Bow: At the end of the lesson, have the child stand and take a bow (see step 4). Then have the student place the guitar in the case. The student should then repeat back to you what he or she is expected to practice during the coming week.

Lesson Two

1. Play the Standing-Still Game.

2. Child Takes a Bow.

3. Learning each other's name (for ages 3–5): Sit on the floor facing the child (or in a circle, if siblings are present). Play the Ball Game (Game No. 3) while singing "Cuckoo" or "Twinkle." Play the guitar, then stop suddenly. When the music stops, the child holding the ball should say his or her name ("Susie," "David," etc.). This is somewhat similar to the game Musical Chairs.

4. Eurythmics: Walk the pulse and sing "Cuckoo" and other songs in Level I. Then clap the pulse while walking. Use rhythm instruments for variety.

5. Sing and clap rhythm syllables.

6. Play Where Is Thumbkin? (ages 3–5).

7. Sing melodic intervals so-mi using the Curwen hand signals.

8. Play the Ready Game (ages 3–8).

9. Review first right-hand position and correct sitting position.

10. Exercise 1 for ages 3–4, **Exercises 1 and 2** for ages 5–6, or **Exercise 3: Walking on the String** for ages 8–10.

11. Play the On-Off Game.

12. Play "Cuckoo" (ages 6–10). It will take many weeks before children ages 3–5 have the necessary coordination to play "Cuckoo" alone. Have patience and lots of praise.

13. Play the Listening Game.

14. Child Takes a Bow.

Lesson Three

Pre-School (Ages 3–5):

1. Review steps in Lesson Two.

2. "Teddy Bear": Chant this song while walking to 2/4 beat. This song is good for learning to follow directions.

> A. Teddy Bear, Teddy Bear, turn around,
> Teddy Bear, Teddy Bear, touch the ground.
>
> B. Teddy Bear, Teddy Bear, touch your nose,
> Teddy Bear, Teddy Bear, touch your toes.
>
> C. Teddy Bear, Teddy Bear, reach up high,
> Teddy Bear, Teddy Bear, touch the sky.

School Age (6–10):

1. Review steps in Lesson Two.

2. If "Cuckoo" has been well learned, continue with "One, Two, Tie My Shoe," "See-Saw," and "Star Light."

3. Technique: Be sure that the student's third left-hand finger is placed behind fret III on string 2. The finger should be well curved, and the fingertip should "look down on the string."

Review Exercise 2. Remind the student to "walk the fingers" (alternate *i, m, i, m*).

Review Exercise 3. Remind the student to use *p* free stroke on strings 5 and 6. Place *i, m, a* on the first three strings to balance the right hand.

4. Have the parent play the first songs. Check posture, hand placement, and technique.

5. Check whether the student is listening to the tape each day.

Lesson Four

Pre-School (Ages 3–5):

1. Review steps in Lesson Two.

2. Walk and sing "Teddy Bear."

3. Introduce Exercise 3.

4. Play Conductor (Game No. 7) and sing Level I songs.

5. Play Thumbkin with Glasses (Game No. 9).

6. Remind the child to listen to the tape at home each day.

7. Switch roles: Let the child become the "teacher" and check whether his or her parent is sitting correctly with the guitar, using good posture and hand positions.

School Age (6–10):

1. Child Takes a Bow.

2. Eurythmics: Walk pulse and sing "Mill Wheel" and "Snail, Snail." Then walk pulse and clap rhythm to "Rain, Rain" and "Ring Around the Rosy." Then use rhythm instruments to tap rhythm while walking.

3. Switch roles: Let the child become the "teacher" and check whether his or her parent is sitting correctly with the guitar, using good posture and hand positions.

4. Introduce Exercise 4: Walking Up and Down the Frets. Place the child's four fingers of the left hand on string 1. Explain that each finger has its own fret. Each finger should be on the exact tip, with finger 1 on fret I, finger 2 on fret II, etc. Do not let the fingers buckle inward. The parent may have to help the child place the fingers accurately at home. With rest stroke, have the child play four counts on F *(i, m, i, m)*, four counts on F♯, etc. Then descend in the same manner. In succeeding lessons, continue on the remaining strings, using the right-hand thumb on strings 5 and 6.

5. Introduce la and play "Snail, Snail."

6. Review Exercise 3.

7. Play the Listening Game (Game No. 6).

Lesson Five

Pre-School (Ages 3–5):

1. **Review steps in Lesson Four.**

2. **Review Exercises 1, 2, and 3.**

3. **Introduce Rhythm Cards** (Game No. 10).

4. **Eurhythmics:** Play the Hand-Clap Game (Game No. 11) to feel the pulse of the music. Children may alternate slapping their knees and clapping their hands while singing Level I songs.

5. **Play the Listening Game** (Game No. 6): While you play **so-mi,** have the child guess (with eyes closed) whether the note is "high" or "low."

6. **Set up a time to discuss with the parents the child's progress and any problems encountered with practicing at home.**

School Age (6–10):

1. **Review steps in Lesson Four.**

2. **Introduce Rhythm Cards** (Game No. 10).

3. **Review Exercises 3 and 4.**

4. **Eurythmics:** Play the Hand-Clap Game (Game No. 11) while singing Level I songs.

5. **Introduce names of strings:** treble = E, B, G; bass = D, A, E.

6. **Do-So Accompaniment:** Have the student play **do-so** on open strings 3 and 4 with rest stroke *(i, m, i, m).*

7. **Set up a time to discuss with the parents any problems with the child's attitude during home practice.**

8. **Check whether the student is listening to the tape each day.**

Imaginative Games, Exercises & Teaching Ideas

Curwen Hand Signals

These signals were developed by John Curwen in 1870. He intended the signals to reinforce the feeling of intervals. They present a visualization in space of the high-low relationship among the notes being sung.

Singing the songs and using the Curwen hand signals are important for the child's musical development and ability to create a beautiful tone.

Ear training and singing intervals are intricately entwined. This is emphasized repeatedly by Kato Havas in *A New Approach to Violin Playing*: *"It is very good practice first to sing the intervals, then to learn to hear them without making any sound at all. [See Imaginative Games No. 12 and 21.] For if the mind is developed to anticipate the right pitch and quality of sound, the fingers will follow the demand of the mind. Instead of spending hours trying to train the fingers to play in tune, we should train our minds to hear the tune."*

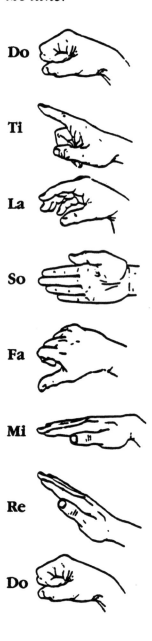

Rhythm Syllables

The rhythm-syllable system is similar to that used in French *solfege;* i.e., the quarter note is "ta" and the eighth note is "ti."

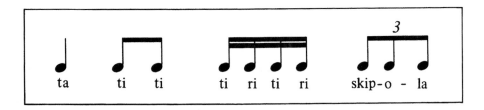

Preliminary Exercises

Exercise 1:

Hold the child's index finger *(i),* the "pointer," and carefully demonstrate a good rest stroke on string 1. Emphasize good tone. Do this a number of times with patience and praise. Then try the same motion with the middle finger *(m),* the "middleman."

a = ring—*annular*
m = middle—*medio*
i = index—*indicio*
p = thumb—*pulgar*

Exercise 2:

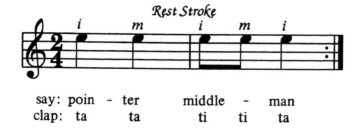

Have the student alternate *i, m, i, m* on string 1 while you say "pointer-middleman" in rhythm. Then have the child clap the rhythm, saying "ta, ta, ti-ti, ta." Then proceed to string 2, alternating *i, m*.

Exercise 3: Walking on the Strings

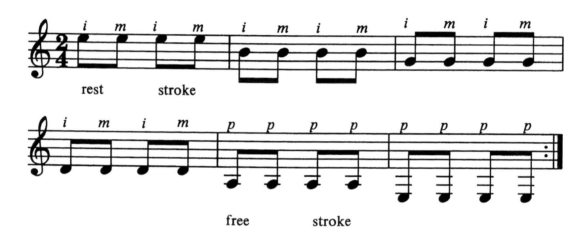

Have the student play *i, m, i, m* on the first four strings, as shown above, with the thumb *(p)* resting on string 5 or 6. Then have the student rest the first three fingers *(i, m, a)* on the first three strings while playing strings 5 and 6 free stroke with the thumb *(p)*. Please emphasize to your young students the importance of creating a beautiful sound. This begins right at the start with playing on the open strings.

Exercise 4: Walking Up & Down the Frets

Rest   Stroke

Place the child's four fingers of the left hand on string 1. Explain that each finger has its own fret. Each finger should be on the exact tip, with finger 1 on fret I, finger 2 on fret II, etc. Do not let the fingers buckle inward. The parent may have to help the child place the fingers accurately at home.

With rest stroke, have the child play four counts on F (*i, m, i, m*), four counts on F♯, etc. Then descend in the same manner.

Continue on the remaining strings, using the thumb (*p*) on strings 5 and 6 with free stroke.

Imaginative Games

1. Standing-Still Game: Have the child assume a pre-bow posture with feet together and hands at the sides. See if the child can stand still to the count of 1–10 without moving. This is important for learning to follow directions.

2. Take a Bow: Have the child stand upright at the count of 1, then bend at the waist at the counts of 2 and 3, and straighten up at the counts of 4 and 5.

3. Ball Game: Sit on the floor opposite the child (or children, if siblings are present). Roll the ball back and forth to the count of 1, 2. Sing easy songs with the child, such as "Cuckoo" or "Twinkle, Twinkle," while rolling the ball back and forth to an even rhythm. This reinforces the feeling of pulse while the child has a good time.

4. Ready Game: Have the child stand about ten feet away from the guitar, which rests in its case. You say, "Ready, get set, go!" and start counting "1, 2, 3, 4, 5," etc., as the child quickly and quietly runs to the guitar case, opens it quickly, removes the guitar, and sits on a small chair with his or her left foot raised on a small footstool and with the guitar held in the correct position. When this is accomplished, the child happily says "Ready!"

5. On-Off Game: First, place a capo on fret VII or V. Place a sticker/star at the third fret on string 2 on the fingerboard to help the child locate **so** in the key of G. Now place the child's left hand on the fingerboard. Count aloud with the child the number of each left-hand finger: "This is finger one, two, THREE." Emphasize naming finger three because small children tend to favor using finger two.

Next, place the child's third left-hand finger just behind the third fret (over the star on the fingerboard) and say "On," then lift the finger off and say "Off." This action should be repeated many times, saying "On-Off."

6. Listening Game: Play the interval **so-mi** (D and B in the key of G) and have the child identify the sounds as "high" or "low." When the child can identify **so** as "high" and **mi** as "low" (either with eyes closed or with back turned to you), tell the child that you will now play three sounds, always starting with **so.** Then the child should sing back to you "high, low, low" or "high, high, low." Eventually the child will be able to distinguish between high and low sounds. When this is well established, you may begin saying the melodic syllables instead of "high" and "low."

7. Conductor: Have the child raise both hands high over his or her head, as if about to conduct an orchestra. Then the child's arms should drop to the side on count 1 and be raised again on count 2. All the beginning songs can be used for this game, which is excellent for developing a strong feeling for the 2/4 pulse.

8. See-Saw Game: Have the child raise his or her arms shoulder high and then move them up and down like a see-saw, while singing any of the beginning songs, especially "See-Saw."

Variation: To stimulate the child's imagination, suggest that you are holding something at the end of the see-saw, such as feathers or bricks. Ask the child to make a suggestion as the what he or she is balancing.

9. Where Is Thumbkin?: This helps the child to "name the fingers." Begin with your hands closed in fists behind your back. On the first stanza, allow your left thumb to come out on "Here I am," and go back on "Run away, Run away." Then repeat the entire procedure, using first the "pointer," then the "middleman," and so on, finally ending with "all of them" (the whole hand).

Variation (Thumbkin with Glasses): With your thumb and pointer make a circle, then repeat with your thumb and middleman, etc. This is a good game for coordination and following directions. And it is especially good for learning the names of the fingers of the right hand *(i, m, a)*.

Where   is Thumb kin?   Where   is Thumb kin?   Here   I   am!   Here   I   am!

How are you   today, sir?   Very well,   I thank you   Run   a - way   Run   a - way

1. Thumbkin	4. Ringman *(a)*
2. Pointer *(i)*	5. Pinkie
3. Middleman *(m)*	6. All of them (whole hand)

10. Rhythm Cards: Mark different rhythm patterns on separate cards and have the child clap the rhythms while saying the rhythm syllables. For example, the following patterns could be used:

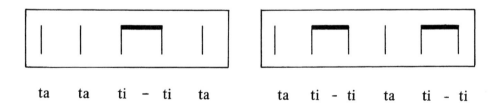

ta   ta   ti - ti   ta   ta   ti - ti   ta   ti - ti

11. Hand-Clap Game: Have the child alternate between knee-slapping and hand-clapping while singing a piece. This is a good game to help the child feel the pulse of the music.

Variation: Have the child clap the pulse (1, 2) while you clap the rhythm.

12. Simon Says: Decide what melodic syllable Simon "will leave out of the song." For example, say to the child, "Simon says to leave out all the **re** syllables while we sing 'All Around the Buttercup.' " Then you and the child use hand signals while singing the song. However, when **re** occurs in the song, the child should sing this silently inside in the "silent language." This is a very good game for listening to sounds accurately and helps to develop the inner ear.

13. Freeze Game: Have the child start to play a piece. When you call out "freeze," the child must stop playing immediately. You then check the child's posture and hand positions. This is an especially good game to play if you wish to correct faulty posture, hand positions, thumb position, etc. It helps the child focus on the problem area while having fun playing a game.

14. Robot: Have the child stand very stiff. The child can move or act only on a verbal order from you; e.g., "Robot raises left foot, ...right foot, ...both hands on head," etc. This helps coordination as well as learning to follow directions.

15. Interview: Have the student continue to play a piece while you conduct an "interview"; e.g., "How many hands do you have? What color are your eyes? What is your friend's name?" etc. The child should be able to answer your questions while playing the piece in correct rhythm. This is a wonderful game to increase concentration.

16. Music Box: Mark all the pieces in Levels I–V on separate squares of colored paper, each level on a different color; e.g., Level I pieces on orange, Level II on green, etc. Put all the pieces in an attractive box. Mix them thoroughly and let the student choose which piece he or she wants to play. If the level of the chosen piece is too advanced, have the child play an ostinato bass accompaniment (**do, so, do, so**), and sing the song together. This is an excellent game for review, and all the children love it.

17. Odd-Even: After your student has completed all Level I pieces and is well into Level II, suggest that he or she begin a daily review of the pieces at home. Pieces with even numbers should be played on even-numbered days; pieces with odd numbers should be played on odd-numbered days. In this manner, the child is constantly reviewing the pieces he or she already knows and continuing to play them more accurately and more musically.

18. Rhythm Sticks: Using colored sticks, colored toothpicks, or Popsicle sticks, arrange a rhythm pattern for the student to clap:

Then gather up the sticks and have the student arrange them on a board, making up a new rhythm pattern. Clap this rhythm together. This is also a good game for workshops.

19. Partner Hand-Clap: In this rhythm game for two or more persons, the partners face each other seated or standing. First clap your own hands, then clap your partner's right hand, then clap your own hands, then your partner's left hand. Keep a steady pulse as you sing the song and clap hands. This game is suitable for an individual lesson or a workshop with several children.

20. Radio: Tilt your hand at an angle to indicate that the "radio is on," and start singing a song with the child. Then, at a certain point in the song, tilt your hand in the opposite direction to indicate that the "radio is off." The child should continue to "sing the song inside in the silent language" until you turn your hand in the other direction to indicate that the "radio is on" again and the child should continue to sing the song aloud. This is an excellent game for workshops.

21. Rhythm Touch-Tap Game: Sing "Twinkle, Twinkle Little Star" while using the melodic syllables. Use a touch-tap rhythm while singing; i.e., tap your knees with your palms and sing **"do-do,"** tap your shoulders and sing **"so-so,"** clap your hands overhead and sing **"la-la,"** then touch your shoulders again and sing **"so-so,"** etc. (see drawing). These same hand motions may be used with any other songs in different rhythms.

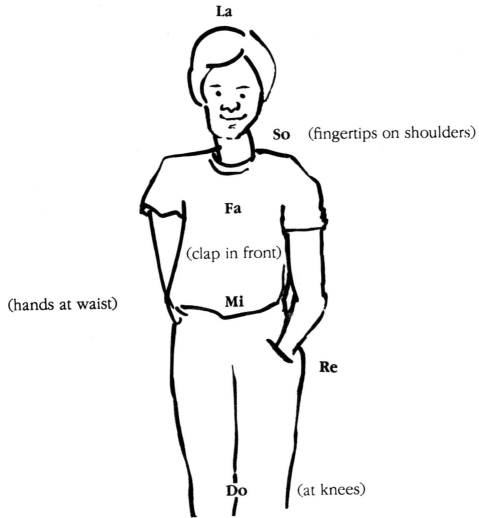

La

So   (fingertips on shoulders)

Fa

(clap in front)

(hands at waist)   Mi

Re

Do   (at knees)

22. What Song Is This?: Play the first phrase of a piece and have the student complete the song. Or hum the first notes of a piece and have the student play the rest. Sometimes, for variety, play "turn-about"—let the student become the "teacher" and play the first few notes of the piece. Children always enjoy this role reversal.

23. Riddle Game: Hold your hand in front of the student, with the back of your hand facing the child and your thumb, index finger, and middle finger together, but separated from the third and fourth fingers. Indicate to the child that the thumb and the first two fingers are **do re mi** and the first two fingers are **so la.** Point with the other hand to each finger as you sing the melody of a song silently, using the correct rhythm. The child follows along by "singing the song silently inside" and then names the song when you have finished. This is excellent for training the child's inner ear and is lots of fun.

24. Leave-It-Out Game: Play a song, such as "Twinkle, Twinkle Little Star" with the student, both of you leaving out one specified note (for example, **fa**) as you both continue to play the song in correct rhythm. The student must follow along carefully and concentrate to be able to do this correctly.

25. Add-a-Note Game: Play a short pattern of notes that the child has not heard before. The student should then play the same pattern immediately afterwards. Then play the same pattern but add one new note. The student should then play the new pattern. Continue until a reasonable number of notes have been added. This game is especially good with several children at workshops.

26. Out-of-Tune Game: Play a piece with deliberately out-of-tune notes. The student should call out every time a sour note is heard.

27. Marble Game: Place some marbles in an attractive box, then ask the student to perform a certain passage that has been difficult for him or her a specified number of times. Each time the student plays the passage well, take one marble from the box. The goal is for the student to perform the passage perfectly several times in a row.

Variation: Ask the student to say how old he or she is and to play the passage that number of times perfectly (e.g., five times for a five-year-old). A marble is "won" each time the student plays well.

28. Follow the Leader: Begin a piece and stop at a certain place in the music. Immediately the student should pick up at that point and continue the piece without a break in rhythm. Then the student should stop playing at a certain point in the music, and you should continue to play the piece. The piece has to continue in the mind and the left-hand fingers of the student when he or she is not actually playing. The beginning game is best played by switching at the end of a phrase. This is a good game to play with several individuals or teams at workshops. You indicate which individual or team is to play next.

29. Right Way/Wrong Way: Play a passage several times and have the child listen closely and tell you if you are playing it the right way or the wrong way each time. This improves a child's attention span, listening ability, and concentration.

30. Grade 1–10: Have the student play a piece with special attention to one aspect of the music; e.g., legato playing. Then ask the student to grade his or her own performance on a scale of 1 to 10. This helps students listen to their own playing with a more critical ear.

31. I Remembered: This game involves repetition to improve a certain passage, posture, hand position, etc. Give the child five chips, and you retain five chips. Then say to the child, "If you remember to keep your fingers down (or sit up straight, or play a passage correctly, etc.) while you play those two measures, then tell me 'I remembered' and I'll give you one of my chips. If you forget, then I get one of your chips. We'll keep playing until one of us gets all the chips."

To "win" the game, the child must execute the skill correctly a number of times consecutively, saying "I remembered" each time.

*Strive to play easy pieces well
and beautifully;
It is better than to render harder
pieces only indifferently well.*

–Schumann–

Level I

1. Cuckoo
2. One, Two, Tie My Shoe
3. See-Saw
4. Star Light, Star Bright
5. Snail, Snail
6. Mill Wheel
7. Rain, Rain
8. Ring Around the Rosy
9. Strawberry Shortcake

I-1. Cuckoo

Focus

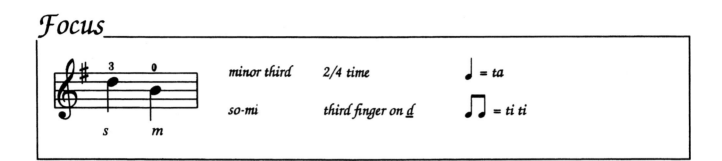

minor third	2/4 time	♩ = ta
so-mi	third finger on *d*	♫ = ti ti

Cuckoo

Folk Song

Cuck - oo   where are you?   Cuck - oo   where are you?

Expansion Activities

A. Play Where Is Thumbkin?: Help the child to "name the fingers." Begin with the hands closed in fists behind your back. On the first stanza allow the left thumb, then the right thumb *(p)* to come out on "Here I am" and go back on "Run away." Go through the motions using a finger for each stanza. (See Game No. 9.)

B. Play the Ball Game: Sit on the floor opposite the child. Roll a ball back and forth to the count of 1, 2, and keep an even rhythm while singing "Cuckoo."

C. Play the Listening Game (see Game No. 6).

I-2. One, Two, Tie My Shoe

One, Two, Tie My Shoe

Folk Song

One, two, tie my shoe, Three four shut the door,
Five, six pick up sticks, Seven, eight, lay them straight,
Nine, ten, a big fat hen, Eleven, twelve dig and delve

Expansion Activities

A. Review Exercise 1. When the child can perform this exercise well, go on to Exercise 2.

B. Play the On-Off Game (Game No. 5).

C. Have the parent hold the guitar in the correct sitting position and then play the intervals **so-mi.** Adjust hand positions as necessary.

D. Sing and play all of the verses of "One, Two, Tie My Shoe" with the child and the parent. Rotate the singing of each verse; i.e., the child sings verse 1, the parent verse 2, and you sing verse 3, etc. This is a good game to involve the parent, and it helps the child learn how to concentrate.

I-3. See-Saw

Focus

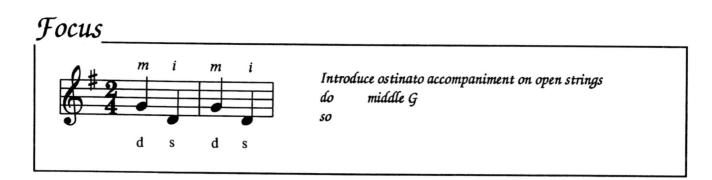

Introduce ostinato accompaniment on open strings
do   *middle G*
so

See-Saw

Folk Song

See   saw   up and down   in the   sky and   on the ground

Expansion Activities

A. Introduce the ostinato accompaniment by having the student play **do-so** on strings 3 and 4. (This is called "playing **do-so** on middle G" to differentiate playing **do-so** on the lowest or bass G on string 6.) The student plays the accompaniment, and you play the melody while you both sing "See-Saw" and then sing "Cuckoo."

Have the student rest the thumb *(p)* on string 5 or 6 while performing this ostinato accompaniment. Ask the student to keep the thumb "ahead of the fingers" or "outside the fingers."

B. Play the See-Saw Game: The child places his or her arms shoulder high and raises them up and down like a see-saw while singing the song to a 1, 2 pulse.

C. Introduce Exercise 3.

I-4. Star Light, Star Bright

Focus

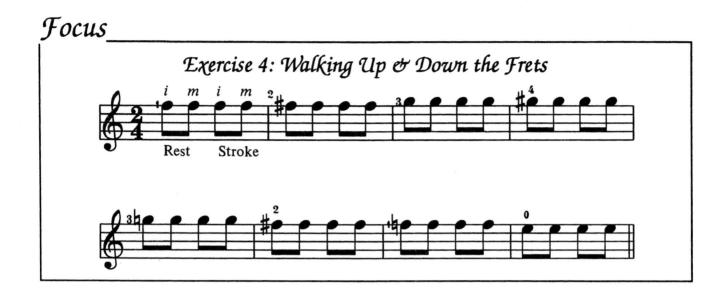

Exercise 4: Walking Up & Down the Frets

Star Light, Star Bright

Folk Song

Star light star bright first star I see to-night

Wish I may, wish I might, have the wish I wish to-night

Expansion Activities

A. Introduce Exercise 4 (see **Imaginative Games, Exercises & Teaching Ideas**).

B. Play the Wishing Game: While playing the Ball Game (Game No. 3), have the student sing "Star Light." When you come to the second line, the child sings out his or her own "wish." For example, the child might sing, "wish I may, wish I might, have a big, red balloon tonight." Try to keep a steady 1, 2 pulse beat with the ball as you sing this song. This is lots of fun to play, and children enjoy using their imagination to make up verses.

I-5. Snail, Snail

Focus

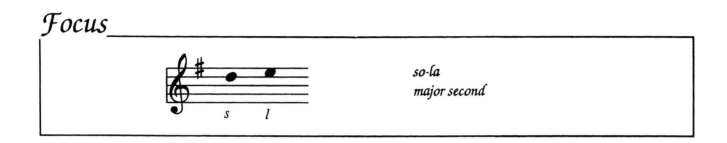

so-la
major second

Snail, Snail

Folk Song

Expansion Activities

Have the student keep the third finger of the left hand on D (third measure) for the first string crossing with the right hand.

I-6. Mill Wheel

Focus

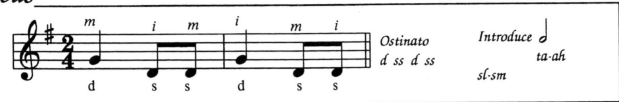

Ostinato
d ss d ss

sl-sm

Introduce 𝅗𝅥
ta-ah

Mill Wheel

Folk Song

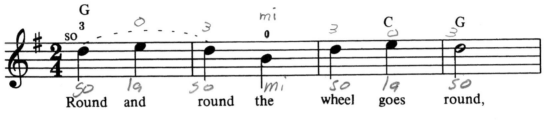

Round and round the wheel goes round,

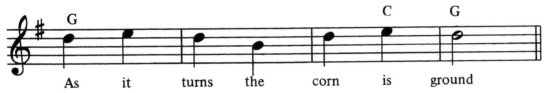

As it turns the corn is ground

Expansion Activities

A. Vary the ostinato accompaniment pattern from **do-so** to **do-so so.** Have the student clap this rhythm before playing on the guitar.

B. Continue to play Where Is Thumbkin? (Game No. 9).

C. While clapping the rhythm to this song, say "ta" for quarter notes and "ta-ah" for half notes.

D. Have the student hold the D in measures 1 and 2.

E. Introduce Rhythm Cards (Game No. 10).

F. Introduce the concepts of loud (ff) and soft (pp). First play the song loud and then soft and have the student echo back to you each phrase.

I-7. Rain, Rain

Focus

Rain, Rain

Rain, Rain, | go - a - way, | come a - gain some | oth - er day
Sun - shine's | here to stay | now we can go | out to play

Expansion Activities

A. When introducing the ostinato accompaniment with the thumb *(p)* playing free stroke, have the student balance the hand by placing the fingers *(i, m, a)* on the first three strings. Watch the right-hand wrist to see that it does not collapse. The third finger of the left hand remains on "bass G" during the accompaniment.

B. Introduce the concept of phrasing. Have the student walk and clap the pulse while singing the song. At the end of measure 2 the student turns and walks in the opposite direction while continuing to clap and sing.

C. Continuously review all the beginning pieces. Sing and play all the pieces with melodic syllables and with the words. (If the child seems reluctant to sing, then you sing the first phrase and have the child respond with the second phrase.)

I-8. Ring Around the Rosy

Focus

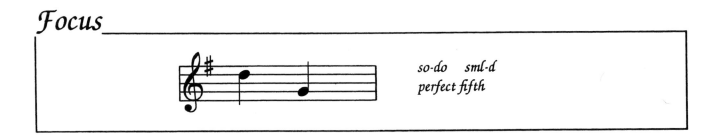

so-do sml-d
perfect fifth

Ring Around the Rosy

Folk Song

Ring a-round the ros - y, pock-et full of pos - y,

Ash - es, ash - es, all fall down.

Expansion Activities

A. Continue to review Exercises 3 and 4.

B. Play the Hand-Clap Game (Game No. 11).

C. Review the Curwen hand signals for all songs. Play Simon Says (Game No. 12).

D. When the student can play the beginning songs easily with confidence, then you can play a **do-so** ostinato or bass-chord accompaniment.

E. The child's wrist should be about 2 inches above the fingerboard. When it starts to sink downward, gently remind the student that "your wrist is a bridge. Let Superman fly under the bridge!" This appeals to young children.

I-9. Strawberry Shortcake

Strawberry Shortcake

American Folk Song

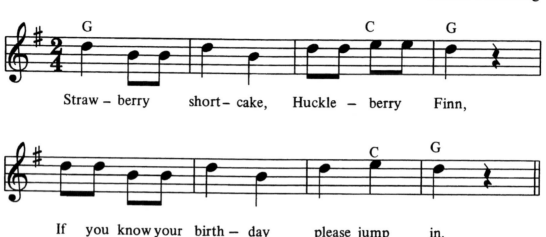

Straw – berry   short – cake,   Huckle – berry   Finn,

If   you know your   birth – day   please jump   in.

Expansion Activities

A. Remind the student to review all the pieces each day at home and to listen to the taped pieces.

B. Have the student try playing the songs with eyes closed. Or have the student play the songs in a dark room.

C. Watch carefully to see that the student places the third finger, left hand, on the exact tip while playing the songs. Also check the alternation of right-hand fingers *(i, m).*

D. Certificate of Merit: If the student can play all the pieces in Level I musically and with ease, he or she earns a Certificate of Merit which is presented at a workshop.

Level II

1. Hot Cross Buns
2. Bye Bye Baby
3. All Around the Buttercup
4. Who's That?
5. Merrily We Roll Along
6. Let Us Chase the Squirrel
7. I See the Moon
8. Bought Me a Cat
9. Rocky Mountain
10. Here Comes Bluebird
11. Fais Do Do
12. Mama, Buy Me a Chiney Doll
13. Twinkle Rhythms
14. Ida Red

II-1. Hot Cross Buns

Focus

mi-re-do
Introduce 4th finger

Hot Cross Buns

Folk Song

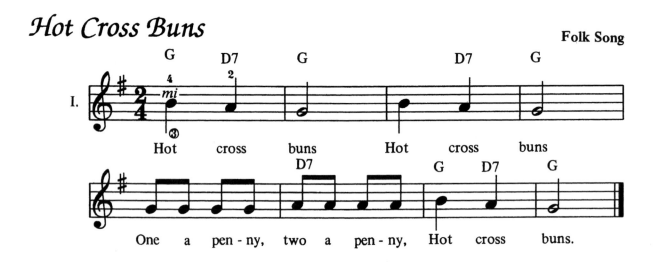

Hot cross buns   Hot cross buns

One a pen - ny, two a pen - ny, Hot cross buns.

ostinato

II.
student
or
teacher

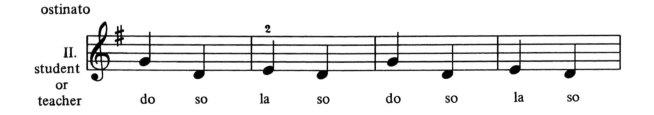

do   so   la   so   do   so   la   so

Expansion Activities

A. Because of the descending line and simple rhythm, "Hot Cross Buns" is a good song for introducing **re** and for using the fourth finger of the left hand on B (**mi**). Have the child play measures 1 to 4 many times before introducing measure 5. The second and fourth fingers should be on exact tips next to the fret.

B. To help students learn to line up the left-hand fingers evenly on the string, have them place all four fingers on the string on the first four frets. Then have the students lift the fingers off the string about a quarter of an inch. Ask them to move the fingers "on" then "off." Do this on all six strings.

C. Play "Hot Cross Buns" on all six strings using the same fingering. Use the free stroke with the thumb *(p)* on strings 5 and 6.

II-2. Bye Bye Baby

Focus

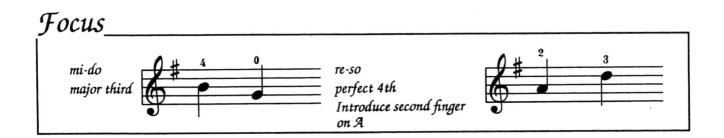

mi-do
major third

re-so
perfect 4th
Introduce second finger
on A

Bye Bye Baby

Folk Song

Bye Bye ba – by ba – by bye

Bye Bye ba – by ba – by bye.

etc.

Expansion Activities

A. Suggest to the student that extra practice is needed in measures 3 and 4. A good idea is to use the Marble Game (Game No. 27) to make repetition more interesting.

B. Play Simon Says (Game No. 12).

C. Continue to review Exercises 3 and 4.

II-3. All Around the Buttercup

Focus

mi-so-re
Reinforce finger coordination
so-re

All Around the Buttercup

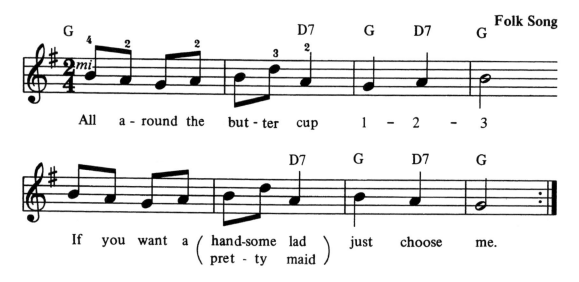

Expansion Activities

A. This is an easy song to sing and an excellent piece for improving finger coordination and independence. Take extra time to help your student with measure 2. In measures 6 and 7 the student should hold the second finger on A.

B. Use this song in a circle game during a workshop. The children form a circle with one child in the center. The children continue walking in a circle while the child in the center points to someone to join him or her. Everyone has a turn in the center of the circle.

II-4. Who's That?

Focus

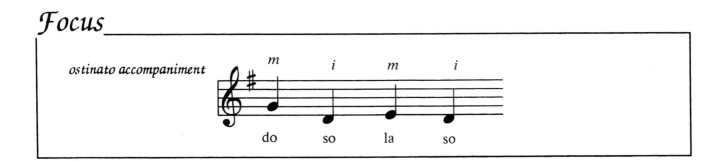

ostinato accompaniment

m   i   m   i

do   so   la   so

Who's That?

Folk Song

Who's that tapp - ing on the win - dow?

Who's that knock - ing on the door?

It's	Michael,	tapping	on	the	window.
It's	Michael,	knocking	on	the	door.
It's	Susie,	tapping	on	the	window.
It's	Maggie	knocking	on	the	door.

Expansion Activities

A. This new ostinato accompaniment introduces the second finger on E (**la**). Also play with "Hot Cross Buns."

B. Sing the rhythm syllables before playing this song. Also play the Hand-Clap Game (Game No. 11).

C. This song is excellent for a workshop. Each child has the chance to leave the group and "tap on the window" and then "knock on the door."

II-5.   Merrily We Roll Along

Merrily We Roll Along

Folk Song

Expansion Activities

A. Remind the student that the second finger remains on A in measure 7. Watch carefully to see that the student uses the fourth finger on B.

B. This is a good song for playing Interview (Game No. 15).

C. Continue to remind the student to listen to the tape at home each day. Stress the importance of a full, round tone.

D. Introduce relative tuning at the fifth fret to the older student, ages 7–10. It is also a good idea to introduce the E minor and E major chords with a simple brush stroke. This will help the student know if the guitar is really in tune and will introduce the concepts of major and minor chords.

E. Continue to review all pieces in Level I and Level II through "Merrily We Roll Along." Have the student play without looking at the fingerboard. Suggest "Let's play this piece while looking at the ceiling" or "Let's play this piece with our eyes closed."

II-6. Let Us Chase the Squirrel

Focus

m r d s   *fast–slow*   *loud (f)–soft (pp)*

Let Us Chase the Squirrel

Folk Song

Let us chase the squir - rel up the hick - 'ry, down the hick - 'ry,

Let us chase the squir - rel up the hick - 'ry tree.

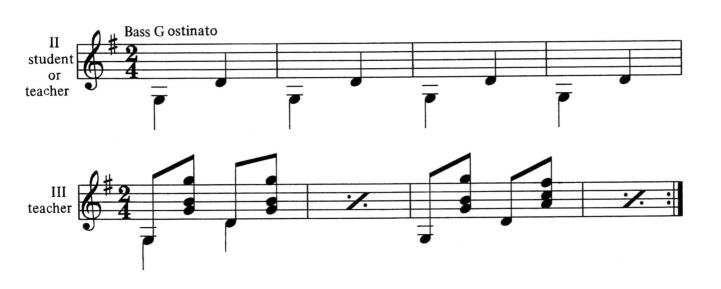

Expansion Activities

A. Have the student retain the second finger on A as the fourth finger reaches for B in measures 3 and 4. This helps to train the left-hand fingers to remain close to the fingerboard.

B. Introduce the concepts of loud (f) and soft (pp) by having the student echo your playing.

C. This is a good piece to show the student differences in tempo. First play the piece fast, then play it very slowly.

D. Have the student play "Hot Cross Buns" while you play "Ring Around the Rosy" as a duet.

II-7. I See the Moon

Focus

s-m-d
Hold third finger on d throughout piece

I See the Moon

Celtic Song

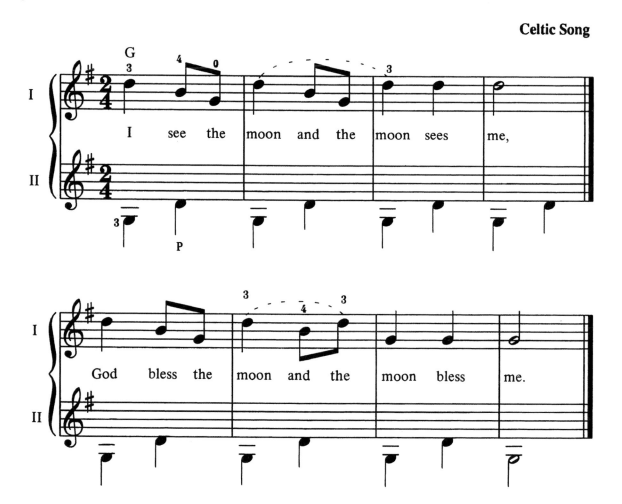

I see the moon and the moon sees me,

God bless the moon and the moon bless me.

Expansion Activities

A. Continue to play Exercise 4: Walking Up and Down the Frets.

B. Introduce Rhythm Sticks (Game No. 18).

II-8. Bought Me a Cat

Bought Me a Cat

Folk Song

Bought me a cat, the cat pleased me.

Fed my cat un - der yon - der tree.

Cat went fid - dle I fee, fid - dle I

fee.
2. Hen went chip - sy chop - sy
3. Duck went sli - shy slo - shy

Expansion Activities

A. Play this song at a lively tempo. Children enjoy adding other animals to the song (cow, dog, sheep, etc.).

B. Play Robot (Game No. 14).

II-9. Rocky Mountain

Rocky Mountain

Folk Song

Rock - y moun-tain, rock -y moun-tain, rock - y moun-tain high.

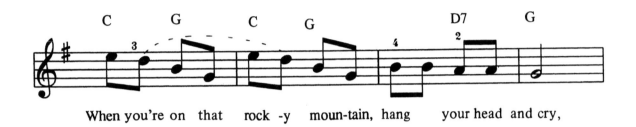

When you're on that rock -y moun-tain, hang your head and cry,

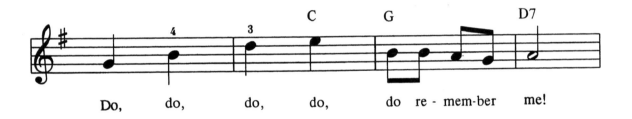

Do, do, do, do, do re - mem-ber me!

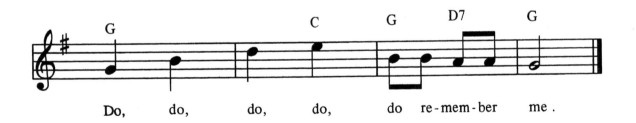

Do, do, do, do, do re-mem-ber me .

Expansion Activities

A. This is a good piece for playing Partner Hand-Clap (Game No. 19).

B. Play this piece by alternating each phrase with your student.

II-10. Here Comes the Bluebird

Here Comes the Bluebird

Folk Song

Here comes the blue - bird, through the win - dow.

Hey did - dle dum - a day day day.

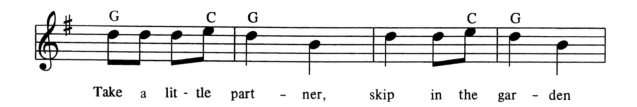

Take a lit - tle part – ner, skip in the gar – den

Hey did - dle dum - a day day day.

Expansion Activities

A. Have the student retain the third finger on D in measures 1–4.

B. Review questions (for the teacher and the parent):
• Is the student listening to the tape at home each day?
• Have the student's posture and hand positions improved?
• Is the student reviewing all the pieces without looking at the fingerboard?

II-11. Fais Do Do

Focus

Introduce **3/4**   *m-r-d*

Fais Do Do

Key of G — Louisiana Folk Song

Fais do - do, and let us go dream - ing.

Fais do - do, come dream - ing with me.

Expansion Activities

A. This French lullaby should be played softly with expression. Since this piece introduces 3/4 time, have the child clap the rhythm before playing on the guitar.

B. Suggest a Home Concert with the child performing for the family at least once a week.

II-12. Mama, Buy Me a Chiney Doll

Focus

Introduce ♫ ti-ri

Mama, Buy Me a Chiney Doll

Folk Song

Ma-ma, buy me a chi-ney doll, Ma-ma, buy me a chi-ney doll,

Ma-ma, buy me a chi-ney doll, do mam-my do!

Expansion Activities

A. Introduce sixteenth-note rhythm by clapping and singing the song before playing on the guitar. It is also a good idea to have the student tap out the pulse on a drum while singing the song.

B. Introduce the "Twinkle Rhythms" (see following page). These rhythms should be introduced a few weeks before playing "Twinkle, Twinkle, Little Star." Have the child clap the rhythm to each variation. When this is well established, have the student play the rhythm on the open G string.

Var. I

skip - o - la, skip - o - la, skip - o - la, skip - o - la,

Var. II

Mis - ter Feb - ru - ar - y, Mis - ter Feb - ru - ar - y,

Var. III

Turn a - gain now turn a - gain, now.

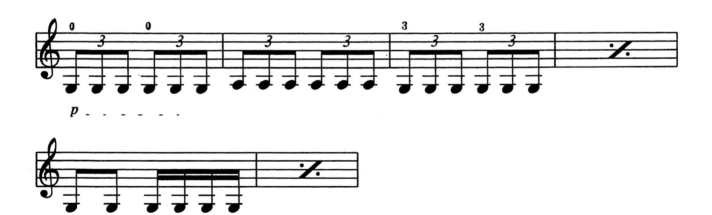

II-14. Ida Red

Ida Red

Folk Song

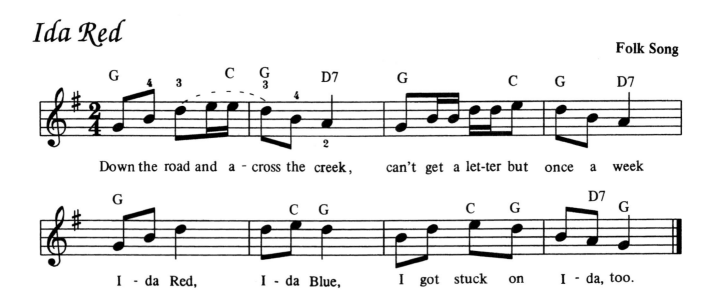

Down the road and a - cross the creek,   can't get a let-ter but once a week

I - da Red,   I - da Blue,   I got stuck on I - da, too.

Duet:

Expansion Activities

A. Have the student listen to his or her own playing by taping the piece during the lesson. Concentrate on listening to good tone.

B. Have the student play Radio (Game No. 20). This game is also quite effective if used in a workshop.

On teaching children:

The greatest duty and joy given to us adults is the privilege of developing our children's potentialities and of educating desirable human beings with beautiful harmonious minds and high sensitivity.

I believe sensitivity and love toward music and art are very important things to all people whether they are politicians, scientists, businessmen or laborers. They are the things that make our life rich.

—Shinichi Suzuki—

Taken separately, too, the elements of music are precious instruments in education.

Rhythm develops attention, concentration, determination and the ability to condition oneself.

Melody opens up the world of emotions. Dynamic variation and tone colour sharpen our hearing.

Singing, finally, is such a many-sided physical activity that its effect in physical education is immeasurable—if there is perhaps anyone to whom the education of the spirit does not matter.

—Zoltan Kodaly—

Music begins where words end.
It is the bridge between
the abstract and the tangible,
between imagination and reality.

—Yehudi Menuhin—

A Man should hear a little music,
read a little poetry and
see a fine picture every day of his life,
in order that worldly cares may not
obliterate the sense of the beautiful
which God implanted in the human soul.

—Goethe—

Level III

1. Twinkle, Twinkle Little Star
2. Aunt Rhody
3. Frere Jacques
4. Lightly Row
5. Hush Little Baby
6. Little River Flowing
7. Michael, Row the Boat Ashore
8. Learning Chords
9. Looby Loo
10. Song of the Wind
11. Lavender Blue
12. Cuckoo, Sing in the Spring
13. Oh, How Lovely Is the Evening

III-1. Twinkle, Twinkle Little Star

Focus

Introduce fa   d r m f s l

Twinkle, Twinkle Little Star

French Folk Song

Twin-kle, twin-kle lit-tle star, How I won-der what you are!

Up a-bove the world so high, Like a dia-mond in the sky,

Twin-kle, twin-kle lit-tle star, How I won-der what you are!

Var. I

skip-o-la

Var. II

Mis-ter Feb-ru-ar-y

Var. III

Turn a-gain now

58

Focus

Play in bass G; hold G throughout piece

Twinkle, Twinkle Little Star

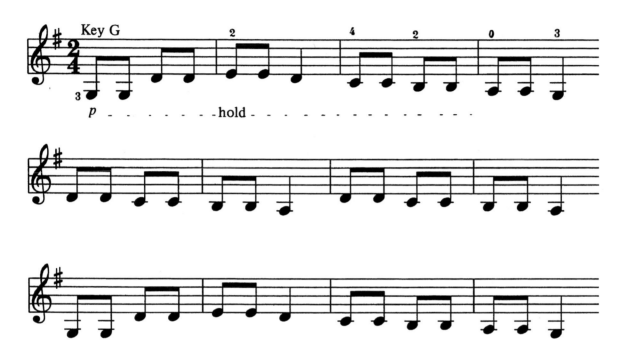

Expansion Activities

A. Fa is introduced for the first time with the use of the proper Curwen hand signal. This is a good song to reinforce the concept of phrasing. You play phrase A, and the student phrase B. For very little children, suggest that "Twinkle" is "like a sandwich"; i.e., phrase A is the "bottom and the top bun," while phrase B is "the hamburger in between."

B. Play the Rhythm Touch-Tap Game (Game No. 21).

III-2. Aunt Rhody

Aunt Rhody

Folk Song

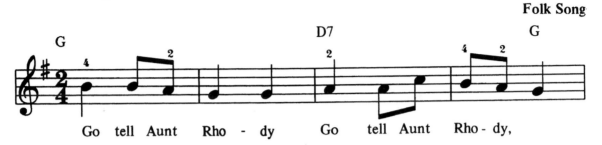

Go tell Aunt Rho - dy Go tell Aunt Rho - dy,

Go tell Aunt Rho - dy, her old gray goose is dead.

2. The one she's been savin' - -
to make a feather bed.

3. She drowned in the mill pond - -
standing on her head.

4. The goslin's are mournin' - -
'cause their mammy's dead.

Expansion Activities

A. Reinforce introduction of **fa** by playing Simon Says (Game No. 12), leaving out the **fa** while singing the melodic syllables.

B. Continue to review all pieces in Level I and Level II. Encourage the student to use the Odd-Even Game (Game No. 17) in review at home.

C. Play What Song Is This? (Game No. 22).

III-3. Frere Jacques

Frere Jacques

Are you sleep-ing? Are you sleep-ing? Broth-er John, Broth-er John,
Frere Jacques   Frere Jacques   Dormez vous,   Dormez vous,

morn-ing bells are ring-ing, morn-ing bells are ring-ing, ding dong ding, ding dong ding.
sonnez les matines, sonnez les matines, din din don, din, din don.

Expansion Activities

A. Play this song three times with the student in a round. This increases the student's ability to concentrate and is a most enjoyable activity.

B. Be careful with right-hand fingering in measure 5. This may take added practice.

C. Review Rhythm Cards (Game No. 10).

III-4. Lightly Row

Focus

Introduce $\frac{4}{4}$ and ABA ternary form

Lightly Row

German Folk Song

Expansion Activities

This piece consists of four phrases of four measures each. It is especially important to sing the words to this longer song. Alternate playing each phrase with your student.

Focus

Introduce sixth   s, mrd

Hush Little Baby

Folk Song

Hush little ba - by   don't say a word,   Ma-ma's gon-na buy you a   mock-ing bird.

2.   If that mocking bird don't sing,
     Mama's going to buy you a diamond ring.

3.   If that diamond ring turns brass,
     Mama's going to buy you a looking glass.

4.   If that looking glass gets broke,
     Mama's going to buy you a billy goat.

5.   If that billy goat won't pull,
     Mama's going to buy you a cart and bull.

6.   If that cart and bull turn over,
     Mama's going to buy you a dog named Rover.

7.   If that dog named Rover won't bark,
     Mama's going to buy you a horse and cart.

8.   If that horse and cart fall down,
     You'll be the*prettiest girl in town.

* (handsomest lad)
  (sweetest little baby)

63

III-6. Little River Flowing

Little River Flowing

Folk Song

Lit - tle riv - er flow - ing, flow - ing, flow - ing,

Lit - tle riv - er flow - ing on-ward to the sea.

Expansion Activities

A. Review "Let Us Chase the Squirrel."

B. Have the child create an original verse; e.g., "When I go to sleep, sleep, sleep, when I go to sleep, then I start to dream," or "When I go to school," etc.

III-7. Michael, Row the Boat Ashore

Focus

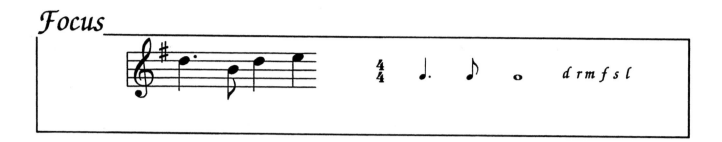

Michael, Row the Boat Ashore

Folk Song

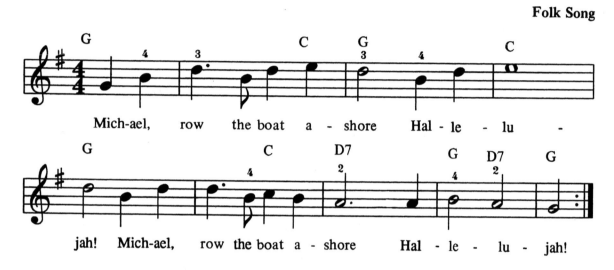

Mich-ael, row the boat a - shore Hal - le - lu -

jah! Mich-ael, row the boat a - shore Hal - le - lu - jah!

Expansion Activities

A. With the introduction of a dotted rhythm, it is good to have the student clap the rhythm before playing on the guitar.

B. Use contrasting musical elements while playing this piece; e.g., vary the tempo from slow to fast, or play very soft (pp) and then loud (f).

C. Play the Riddle Game (Game No. 23).

III-8. Learning Chords

Simple Thumb Brush

Strings 1, 2, 3

Cuckoo
I See the Moon
One, Two, Buckle My Shoe
Ring Around the Rosy

	I G	IV	V7

Snail, Snail
Strawberry Shortcake   G
Rain, Rain

C

Bye Bye Baby
Bought Me a Cat
Hot Cross Buns   G
Go Tell Aunt Rhody
Hush Little Baby
Little River Flowing

D7

Michael, Row the Boat Ashore
Rocky Mountain   G   C   D7
Twinkle, Twinkle Little Star

All six strings

Shalom
Zoom Gali Gali   Em

I

IV   V

Am

Older children enjoy learning to play a few simple chords using brush stroke with the thumb.

✺ **The first group** of songs uses only the G chord on the first three strings.

✺ **The second group** uses G and adds and C chord.

✺ **The third group** uses G and D7. (Note: To play D7 easily, have the student glide the third finger of the left hand along string 1 from G to F♯. Then place the first and second fingers on C and A.)

✺ **The fourth group** uses all three chords: G, C, and D7.

Since the student already knows how to sing and play the songs, it is fairly easy to learn a simple accompaniment.

III-9. Looby Loo

Focus

Introduce $\frac{6}{8}$ ♩.

Looby Loo

Folk Song

Here we dance Loo - by Loo, Here we dance Loo - by Light,

Here we dance Loo - by Loo, all on a Sat - ur-day night.

Expansion Activities

A. A good way to introduce 6/8 time to your student is to think in terms of two beats to a measure. Place a rope or a ruler on the floor and have the child clap three beats on one side of the rope and then three beats on the other side; i.e., "step, clap, clap—step, clap, clap." When the rhythm is firmly established, have the child sing the song while clapping and stepping over the line.

B. Continue to emphasize the importance of listening. Have students listen carefully to their own playing by using a tape recorder in your studio. The sound will tell the students whether they are doing well. If the sound is harsh or unpleasant, stop and check. Then begin again.

III-10. Song of the Wind

Focus

Legato playing: Hold first finger down on C in measures 1 to 7.

Song of the Wind

Words: S. Michelson
Folk Song

See the love - ly au - tumn leaves Blow - ing in the

wind, blow – ing in the wind. See them swirl – ing,

see them twirl – ing, Drift – ing in the au – tumn blue.

See them swirl – ing, see them twirl – ing Just for me and you.

Expansion Activities

A. It is important to clap the rhythm to this piece before playing on the guitar. Clap the pulse and have the student clap the rhythm. Especially watch the half notes in measures 4 and 6, and have the student hold for the full count.

B. Emphasize smooth legato playing with expressive dynamics and a full, round tone.

III-11. Lavender Blue

Focus

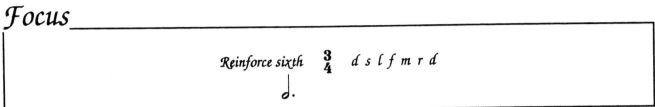

Reinforce sixth $\frac{3}{4}$ d s l f m r d

Lavender Blue

Folk Song

Lav - en - der blue dil-ly, dil-ly, lav - en - der green,

If I am king dil-ly, dil- ly, you shall be queen.

Expansion Activities

A. Continue to review all pieces in Levels I–III.

B. Suggest that your student attend concerts and listen to classic guitar records and tapes.

C. Play the Leave-It-Out Game (Game No. 24).

III-12. Cuckoo, Sing in the Spring

Focus

Reinforce   **3/4**   𝅘𝅥𝅮.   s f m r d

Cuckoo, Sing in the Spring

Austrian Folk Song

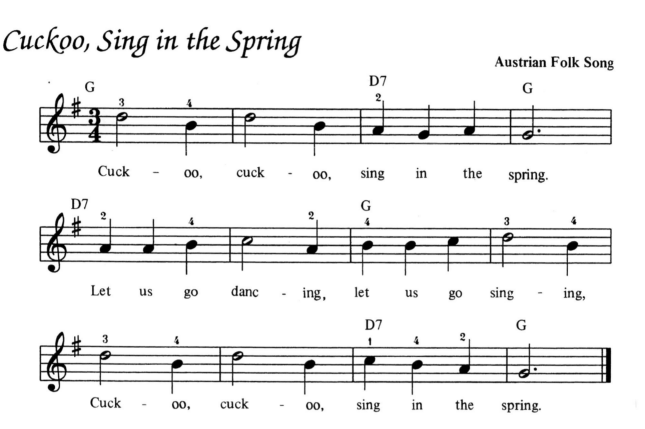

Cuck - oo, cuck - oo, sing in the spring.

Let us go danc - ing, let us go sing - ing,

Cuck - oo, cuck - oo, sing in the spring.

Expansion Activities

A. Have the student play the piece with contrasting musical elements; e.g., loud (f) then soft (pp).

B. Play the Add-a-Note Game (Game No. 25).

C. Play Right Way/Wrong Way (Game No. 29).

III-13. Oh, How Lovely Is the Evening

Oh, How Lovely Is the Evening

Canon - England

Expansion Activities

A. When this piece is well learned, have the student play it three times as a round. This is a lovely piece to play and will help improve the student's ability to concentrate.

B. Play the Leave-It-Out Game (Game No. 24).

Level IV

1. May Song
2. Jim Along Josie
3. Come Little Children
4. Simple Gifts
5. Moon Magic
6. Love Somebody
7. Sometimes I Hear a Song
8. English Song

IV-1. May Song

May Song

Folk Song

Expansion Activities

A. Have the student hold the third finger on D in measures 1 and 2. Emphasize dynamics and expressive playing using a full, round tone.

B. Remind the student to continue listening to the tape at home.

C. Try playing a duet with "May Song" and "Twinkle, Twinkle Little Star."

IV-2. Jim Along Josie

Focus

Different rhythms: walk, hop, march, run
slow–fast
s m d l

Jim Along Josie

Oklahoma Dance Song

Hey! Jim a - long Jim a long Jo - sie! Hey, Jim a - long Jim a-long Joe!

2. Hey walk along, Jim - along Josie
   Hey walk along Jim along Joe.
3. hop
4. swing
5. roll
6. march
7. jump
8. run

Expansion Activities

A. Have the student walk, hop, jump, and march to the song while you play the guitar. When the various rhythms are well established, have the student learn to play each one on the guitar. This is an excellent piece to use in workshops. The children will enjoy themselves greatly.

B. It is a good idea to put one or two pieces from Level IV on an endless three-minute tape for repeated listening at home.

IV-3. Come Little Children

Come Little Children

Words: Erica Colleton
Music: Johann Schulz (1747-1800)

O come lit – tle chil – dren and play in the sun . O come lit – tle chil – dren while you are still young. The years may pass, and the mem – or – ies will fade, but still you'll re – mem-ber your child-hood play.

Expansion Activities

A. Play only one phrase at a time with your student. Have him listen very carefully to both tone and dynamics with emphasis on legato playing.

B. Record the student while he is playing this piece in the studio. Then have the student listen critically to his or her own performance.

IV-4. Simple Gifts

Focus

Introduce ti

Simple Gifts

18th Century Shaker Hymn

Expansion Activities

A. The student will need extra practice in measure 4. Be sure the fourth finger is just behind the fret on the very tip of the finger.

B. Play Follow the Leader (Game No. 28).

IV-5. Moon Magic

Focus

> Introduce key am   l d m l
> Use p throughout song

Moon Magic

Sonia Michelson

Words: Christine Kelly

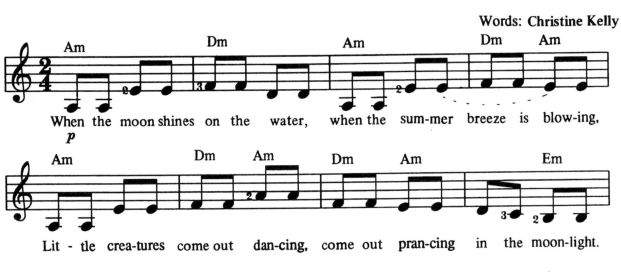

When the moon shines on the water, when the sum-mer breeze is blow-ing,

p

Lit - tle crea-tures come out dan-cing, come out pran-cing in the moon-light.

When the moon shines on the wa-ter there's a spe - cial kind of mag - ic,

Lit - tle crea-tures that were hid - ing come out once a - gain to play.

Expansion Activities

This is the first piece written in a minor key with the melody played free stroke with the thumb. Emphasize good tone while playing on the bass strings.

IV-6. Love Somebody

Focus

Reinforce ti—with fourth finger
d r m f s ti s

Love Somebody

Love some bod - y? "Yes I do!" Love some-bod-y? "Yes I do!"

Love some bod -y? "Yes I do! Love some - bod-y, but I won't say who!"

Expansion Activities

A. Pay extra attention to measure 4. The F♯ should be clear, with the finger well curved.

B. Suggest that the student play with eyes closed or with the room dark.

C. Play the Leave-It-Out Game (Game No. 24).

Sometimes I Hear a Song

Words: Christine Kelly
Sonia Michelson

Some - times I hear a song la, la, and
sing it all day long tra - la, I
sing it in the bath tra - la, and
hum it dur - ing math la, la.

2. While going home for lunch, la, la
   And during every munch, tra, la
   I have to sing my song, tra, la
   Or feel that something's wrong, la, la.

3. When school is finally out, la, la,
   I sing it with a shout, hurrah
   At dinner it is snuffed, tra, la
   Because my mouth is stuffed, la, la.

4. The oddest thing to me, la, la
   And see if you agree, tra, la
   Oh my! - - the song next day, tra, la
   Is completely gone away, la, la.

Expansion Activities

Have the student play this piece at a brisk tempo. The student will have a good time learning to sing the words, and this tune will also increase the student's awareness of melody.

IV-8. English Song

Focus

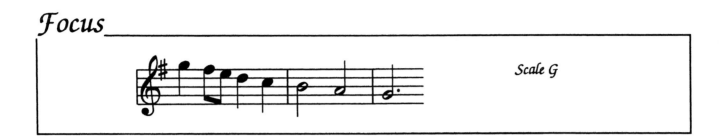

Scale G

English Song

English Folk Song

Expansion Activities

A. Have the student pay extra attention to the rhythm in measures 6 and 7.

B. Play the Marble Game (Game No. 27).

This page has been intentionally left blank.

To be a teacher
is to have a great responsibility.
The teacher helps shape and give
direction to the lives of
other human beings.
What is more important, graver, than that?

Children and young people are
our greatest treasure.
when we think of them
we think of the future of
the world.

—Pablo Casals—

The guitar's timbre
possesses a natural
melancholy, something
intrinsic.
The charm seems to come
from mysterious distances
and to touch profound
resonances in the soul.

—Andres Segovia—

Music, poetry, religion
they all initiate in the soul's
encounter with an aspect of
reality for which reason has no
concepts and language has no names.

Music does not describe that which is,
rather it tries to convey that which
reality stands for.
The Universe is a score
of Eternal Music, and we are
the cry,
we are the voice.

—Abraham Heschel—

Level V

1. I'll Be a King
2. Turn Again, Whittington
3. Cotton Eye Joe
4. Baker's Shop
5. Five Hundred Miles
6. Round Up Four
7. Alabama Girl
8. Who Built the Ark?
9. Green Holm Jig
10. Freight Train
11. Minuet —W. A. Mozart
12. Minuet in G —J. S. Bach

V-1. I'll Be a King

Focus

$\frac{3}{8}$ *Reinforce sixth*   d r m f s l   ti

I'll Be a King

S. Michelson
Words: C. Kelly

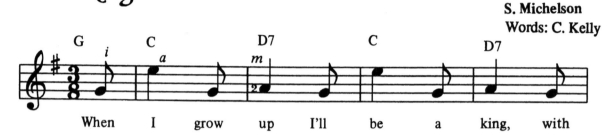

When   I   grow   up   I'll   be   a   king,   with

gold – en   crown   and   dia – mond   ring,   and

fur   trimmed cloak,   all   in   bright   red,   I'll

be   a   king   sweet   Su – sie   said.

2. Oh no, her brother spoke right up,
   With golden crown or silver cup
   Or fur-trimmed cloak all in bright red,
   You can't be king, her brother said.

3. What's that you say, she asked with a sigh,
   Is it something else that girls can't try?
   With golden crown and scepter blue
   I'll be as good a king as you!

4. That's not the point, her brother said.
   Recall your history and what you've read?
   We've no kings since the British came and went,
   So you'll have to make do with President!

V-2. Turn Again, Whittington

Focus

Turn Again, Whittington

Turn a-gain Whit-ting-ton turn a-gain Whit-ting-ton

thou wor-thy ci-ti-zen Lord ma-yor of London.

Expansion Activities

A. Write out the music on staff paper and have the student clap the dotted rhythm before playing the piece on the guitar.

B. Play Right Way/Wrong Way (Game No. 29).

C. Play Interview (Game No. 15).

V-3. Cotton Eye Joe

Cotton Eye Joe

Folk Song

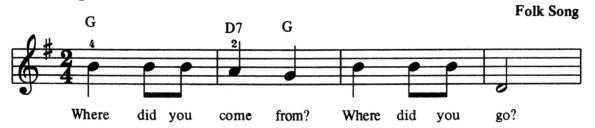

Where did you come from? Where did you go?

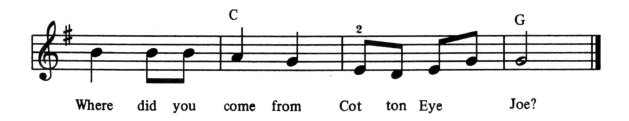

Where did you come from Cot ton Eye Joe?

> 2.　Come for to see you, come for to sing,
> Come for to show you my diamond ring.

Expansion Activities

A. Emphasize legato playing and good expression.

B. Play Simon Says (Game No. 12).

C. Play Radio (Game No. 20).

V-4. Baker's Shop

Focus

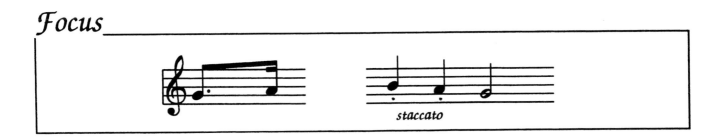

staccato

Baker's Shop

Down to the bak - er's shop. Hop, hop, hop.

For my moth er said, "Buy a loaf of bread."

Down to the bak - er's shop. Hop, hop, hop.

Expansion Activities

A. Write out this dotted rhythm on staff paper and have the student clap the rhythm before playing the piece.

B. Introduce staccato in measure 2 with careful right-hand placement.

V-5. Five Hundred Miles

Focus

Introduce slur descending

Five Hundred Miles

Folk Song

do

If you miss the train I'm on, you will know that I am gone

you can hear the whistle blow – a hundred miles_____ a

(200 miles)
(300 miles)

Chorus

hundred miles a hundred miles a hundred miles a hundred miles.

2. two hundred miles
3. three hundred miles etc.

Expansion Activities

A. Introduce the descending slur in measure 6 with special attention to left-hand finger placement.

B. The student will enjoy singing all the words to this song, and it is an excellent piece to use at workshops.

V-6. Round Up Four

Focus

Introduce syncopation

Round Up Four

Folk Song

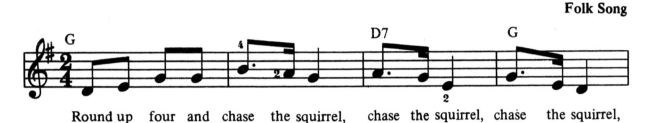

Round up four and chase the squirrel, chase the squirrel, chase the squirrel,

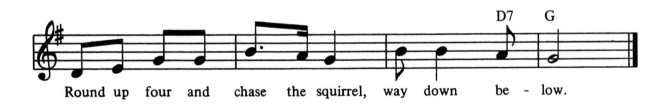

Round up four and chase the squirrel, way down be - low.

Expansion Activities

A. Syncopation is introduced for the first time in measure 7. It is a good idea to clap the rhythm for the entire piece before having the student play it on the guitar.

B. Play What Song Is This? (Game No. 22).

V-7. Alabama Girl

Focus

alla breve   𝄵   *Reinforce syncopation*

Alabama Girl

Folk Song

Al – a – ba – ma girl won't you come out to - night,

come out to – night, come out to–night? Al – a - ba - ma girl won't you

come out to - night and dance by the light of the moon.

Expansion Activities

A. Clap ♪ ♩ ♪ ♩ which first appears in measure 2.
      ti ta ti ta-ah

B. Play Grade 1–10 (Game No. 30).

C. Continue to review pieces (Games 16 and 17).

V-8. Who Built the Ark?

Focus

Reinforce syncopation
Introduce damping
Introduce seventh

Who Built the Ark?

Jamaican Spiritual

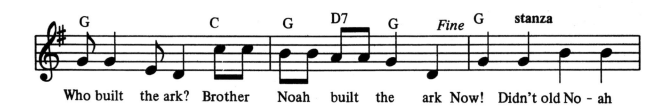

Who built the ark? No - ah, No - ah,

Who built the ark? Brother Noah built the ark Now! Didn't old No - ah

Build the ark? He built it out of a hick- or - y bark.

2. Built it long, both wide and tall,
    Plenty of room for the large and small.

Expansion Activities

A. Introduce damping with the right hand in measure 1.

B. Play Radio (Game No. 20).

V-9. Green Holm Jig

Green Holm Jig

Folk Song

Expansion Activities

A. Be sure to clap this 6/8 rhythm before playing this piece.

B. Encourage a good tempo after the piece is learned. Watch the sixteenth notes in measure 9.

V-10. Freight Train

Freight Train

Elizabeth Cotton

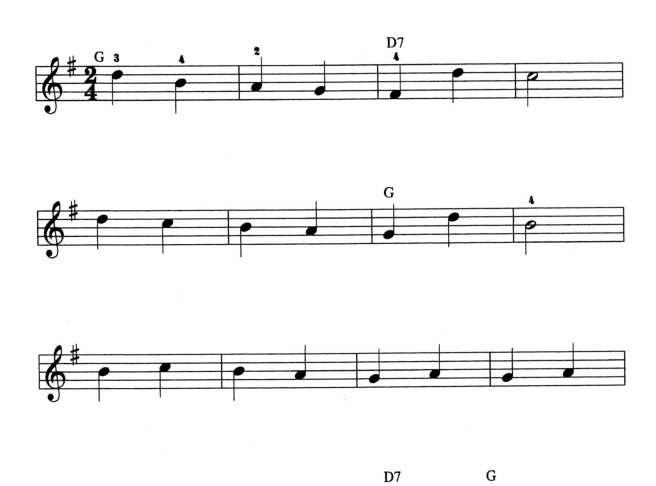

Expansion Activities

Play I Remembered (Game No. 31).

V-11. Minuet

Minuet

W. A. Mozart
(1756 - 1791)

Expansion Activities

This charming little minuet should be played with grace and ease. Please pay particular attention to the rhythm and fingering in the middle section.

V-12. Minuet in G

Minuet in G

J. S. Bach
(1685 - 1750)

Expansion Activities

A. The emphasis in this piece is on good musical phrasing. The end of each phrase should be played softly.

B. Help the student to achieve a full, round tone and legato playing.

C. Play Follow the Leader (Game No. 28).

For additional solo material, see Sonia Michelson's *Easy Classic Guitar Solos for Children,* available through Mel Bay Publications, Inc., #4 Industrial Drive, Pacific, MO 63069. Toll free 1-800-8 MEL BAY (1-800-863-5229) or **www.melbay.com**.